We Want Mashgiach Now!

· ·

Tales of a Kosher Cop

· ·

Allan Lieberman

KOSHERCOP18@gmail.com

www.koshercop.net

This book is dedicated to

Rabbi Moshe Scheiner

Palm Beach Synagogue

He recognized something in me and
provided the encouragement and motivation
to become a Mashgiach

and my dear wife

Ellena "Chava Leah" Lieberman

Whose faith, belief and trust in me allowed
this book to become a reality and for
noodging me to take the Mashgiach Course

Special Thanks to

Rabbi Manis Friedman

When asked for his input as to whether I should continue working as a Mashgiach he responded: "Do you want to be a cop?"

Without his sagacious advice there would not have been a subtitle

Baruch Hashem

Who creates everything

Who gives life & sustains us

TABLE OF CONTENTS

Introduction

For years I've been thinking about documenting my experiences as a Kosher Cop. Yes, That's how I view the work of a Mashgiach, an enforcer of Kashrut, Kosher law. The police cars in my home town, Chicago, have these words written on them: We Serve and Protect. Both police and Mashgichim are shomrim, Hebrew for protectors. Cops protect people from being killed. Mashgichim protect Jews from eating non-Kosher, a very serious issue.

A **Mashgiach**, literally "supervisor," is a Jewish person who supervises the kashrut status of a kosher establishment. A Mashgiach may supervise any type of a Kosher food service establishment, including slaughterhouses, food manufacturers, hotels, caterers, nursing homes, restaurants, butchers, groceries, or cooperatives. The Mashgiach usually works as the on-site supervisor and inspector, representing a kosher certification agency or a local rabbi, who actually makes the policy decisions for what is certifiably Kosher.

A Mashgiach's work is straight forward. It consists of checking certain fruits and vegetables for bugs, checking to see that all ingredients used in food preparation carry an acceptable Kosher hashgacha, (certification) and making sure that meat vessels and utensils are used in the preparation of meat dishes and that dairy vessels and utensils the same. Pareve (neither milk or meat) food preparation requires equal watchfulness.

Checking for bugs can be quite tedious especially when you're not finding any. In fact I have often felt as if I am an abject failure if I come up bugless in a bag of Romaine Lettuce, a bunch of broccoli or a stalk of celery. In order to overcome these feelings of inadequacy I have derived a different way of looking at these matters: I fashion myself as The Great White Hunter embarking on a Bug Hunting Safari. Instead of Rhinos and Water Buffalo it is thrips and aphids I seek. I may not find any but I have put up the good hunt and have done my best. In addition, great solace is gained by knowing that many people go on deep sea fishing excursions and come up with nary a nibble on their line. As my old friend Tony Baker says: This is why they call it fishing, not catching.

Other venues are events where a Kosher Caterer provides the food. Many times there is some preparation to be done at the event and the Mashgiach's job is the same as in a restaurant. Often there is no preparation required and there are other things to look out for. This may include checking shopping bags which have been used by event attendees to smuggle in Grandpa's favorite single malt scotch which does not bear a Kosher symbol. This can be extremely dangerous. (Chapters 4-5)

Much of my work as a Mashgiach can be compared to that of a Substitute Teacher. In this capacity I have filled in for Mashgichim who have called in sick, gone on vacation or just want to take some time off. As a result I have worked at quite a few Kosher Caterers and Kosher Restaurants in S. Florida.

Whenever I work at a new facility I always introduce myself to the owner and staff in this way: "Hello, I'm Allan. I'll be working here as the Mashgiach for the next few days, week(s)." I might as well have said: Shalom, I'm Isser Shlomo Ben Pesach because they're either going to call me Rabbi or Mashgiach. 100% GUARANTEED. There's not much to be said for formal introductions. Most of the owners and staff where I work call me Rabbi. Allow me to theorize as to why this is so. Perception can be reality. My yarmulke, beard and tzitzis would cause many people to assume I am a Rabbi. But that's not why I'm called Rabbi. Here's why: they can't pronounce Mashgiach. The Hebrew pronunciation of *CH* does not exist in the English language. We say chicken, watch, charisma. The glottal Hebrew *CH* is a tough one, even for some people who can speak Hebrew. It's all about fear--fear that utterance of the Hebrew *CH* sound could result in some phlegm popping from one's mouth.

So let's just make it easy on ourselves and we'll call him Rabbi.

Mashgiachim who work at a restaurant split their time between the kitchen and the dining area. It's a good idea to show his or her face so the customers can see that there is a Kosher Cop on the premises. While spending time on the restaurant floor the Mashgiach can mingle amongst the customers and schmooze with them. Often a customer has a question about the Hashgacha of the beef, chicken, turkey or lamb being used. Most times this is a legitimate request as the customer prefers one Hashgacha over another. Other times the person asking the questions is putting on a dog and pony show for his dining party. This is what I mean:

Once I was checking vegetables in the kitchen when a waiter came and asked me to step out to the floor to address the questions of a customer. The conversation went like this: "Hello, I'm Allan Lieberman, the Mashgiach. How may I help you?"

"Who has the Hashgacha here?" the customer inquired.

"ORB."

"What's ORB?"

"Orthodox Rabbinical Board"

"I never heard of them"

"Don't feel bad, they probably never heard of you"

I got smiles from the other members of this dining party but not   from the interrogator.

"What about the meat and chicken......whose Hashgacha is it?"

"All meat is Shor Habor and the chicken is CHK"

"Are you sure?"

"When I came to work an hour ago it was but I can check again if you like."

"Yes, I would appreciate that."

"Would you care to join me?"

Unfortunately he declined. Had he accepted I was prepared to offer him a parka. I would have explained to him this is so he wouldn't freeze to death because we keep our walk-in freezer at a brisk 40 degrees below zero. That's so in case of a power outage it would take 3-4 days for everything to defrost and we could probably sell it out before then. This was the kind of guy who took himself way too seriously. Maybe he took me seriously too.

Back to the kitchen. Outside of the Chef and cooking staff most of the kitchen help in the venues I have worked in are either of Haitian or Hispanic origin. Sometimes this can be detrimental to effective communications.

One day I reported to work at a Restaurant. My first task was to wash Romaine Lettuce. One of the sinks in the "washing station" had been used to wash dishes, pots and pans and needed to be cleaned. So I asked the dishwasher if he could wash the sink so I could proceed. He nodded approval.

Shortly thereafter I returned and found the dishwasher sitting comfortably in a chair beside the sink which had not been cleaned. I pointed to the sink and said: "So.....nu?" I'm certain he had no idea what I just said but he could read body language. "I wash the sink, I wash it" he replied. "Sure don't look like it" I mumbled under my breath. Realizing that a 3rd party was required I asked Pierre to help out. He was informed of my request and spoke to Jean. Jean replied. Pierre giggled.

"Rabbi..... Jean said you asked him to WATCH the sink."

Wash.......watch.......whatever.

Another time, same restaurant, one of the kitchen staff approaches me and says, "The chef want you." So I walk out and asked the chef what he wanted. He just looked at me with a quizzical look and asked what made me think I was needed. I informed him that Jean, yes, the same Jean who watched the sink, told me you requested my presence. "Rib Eye Rib Eye" he exclaimed "I told him to bring me some RIB EYE and he brings me some RABBI." Deep down inside I felt that the chef was grateful that Jean didn't bring him just ANY Rabbi, not just SOME Rabbi, but most definitely a Rabbi who is also a Mashgiach. One must thank the Lord above for small favors.

Chapter 1
In The Beginning

In April of 2012 I became a Mashgiach. My certification was issued by ORB in South Florida. As part of my training I was sent to various restaurants and caterers to experience different situations with different challenges. In my eagerness to get this experience I accepted almost everything offered to me.

My first trial was at a catering "facility." I drove an hour and a half to get there Motzei Shabbos (Saturday night) and worked from 10:00 PM until 5:00 AM. This makeshift location was in a dingy, dirty warehouse with no running water and sparse lighting. It was a transitory facility being used until their new building under construction was complete.

Upon arrival I was given my first task which was washing a case of Romaine Lettuce. Being a newcomer I brought along my manual which explained the procedures for checking vegetables for bugs. For Romaine you need (1) a vessel to put the lettuce in; (2) water to fill the vessel; (3) vegetable wash or a detergent to be mixed in the water; (4) a spinner to remove water from the leaves and (5) a light box to check for bugs. They were missing all but one of the essential items. The only thing they had was water. It wasn't running water, it was rain water which had been collected into buckets from the leaking roof.

By the time I got started it was too late to call any of the ORB Rabbis to find out how to handle this. I was on my own. My first inclination was to find out what else needed to be checked for bugs. Fortunately there was nothing else. So I formulated my strategy.

There are approximately 25-30 leaves on an average head of Romaine Lettuce. There are 3 heads in a bag and 12 bags in a case. That makes for 1,260 leaves of lettuce. Accounting for a break and 1 or 2 trips to the bathroom, I had 6 hours to wash the lettuce. That broke down to 210 leaves washed per hour which meant 3.5 leaves per minute.

With the calculations out of the way I had to figure out how to wash the lettuce and then where to put it. There was only one way to wash the lettuce: do it in the buckets of rainwater for that's all I've got! And how do I check for bugs? That's easy…look at each leaf individually and hold it up to the light. And where do I find a light in this dark, dingy place? Voila! I've got a flashlight on my phone. And how do I dry the lettuce? Ya got me there, can't expect everything! Finally, where do I put the lettuce? No problem, back in the bag where it came from.

Glad to say I never worked there again.

One of the perks of being a substitute Mashgiach is that you get to eat at different restaurants. Most restaurants will offer you something to eat. Some don't, however, and so one must learn their way around the kitchen. By this I mean you must recognize the ample opportunities to "chop a nosh," (there's that *CH* again) that is to grab a taste of whatever is available for the tasting. Allow me to explain.

Smoked chicken tacos were on the menu at a restaurant where I worked. At smaller restaurants where there is not a lot of vegetable washing a Mashgiach is often asked to help out in different ways. I was asked to pull the smoked chicken off the bone one day. So I began plucking the meat from the bone, placing the succulent mesquite smoked chicken into the bowl.

The temptation to pop a pulkeh (leg) into my mouth became too great to bear and so I procured a plate for myself. I designated it as my "personal pullet pushke." After completing 2-3 chickens I indulged in the fruits of my labor. This had to be done in a clandestine manner. Sneaking food and consuming it without detection became another one of my specialties.

A new restaurant opened which specialized in creative exotic salads and was also known for having the premier Sushi Chef in South Florida. It became so popular that you needed to make a reservation for lunch. The Mashgiach on the 1st shift quit suddenly and I was asked to cover it for a few days. In my eagerness to try the faire at this popular restaurant I accepted.

The Rabbi who recruited substitute Mashgichim provided whatever information I needed to know. He asked if I had any questions.

"No, you covered everything that's pertinent.. But I'm curious as to why the previous Mashgiach left in a huff. Do you know why?"

What I learned caused a bit of consternation. The Mashgiach had gotten into a verbal scuffle with the Sushi Chef who proceeded to threaten him with his sushi knife. The Rabbi explained that the Mashgiach's life passed before his eyes, he got nauseous and submitted his resignation effective on the spot.

"So, you're sending me into a war zone with Samurai Sushi Dude? In case I get slashed am I covered by Workmen's Compensation? Can I check first to see if my life insurance covers an untimely demise such as this? Can you hire an off duty cop to accompany me?"

After the Rabbi allayed all my concerns he suggested that I should not engage Psycho Sushi Man in conversation. "Oh yeah? And what if I catch him using Mock Crab and there's nothing mock about it at all? Or eel sauce made from freshly smushed eel? What do I do then?"

"Calm down Allan. You just call us if there's any problem."

Unwilling to run the risk of developing a reputation as a prima donna I took the gig.

Upon my arrival I went straight to the kitchen to see what needed to be washed. All they needed at the moment was some herbs and some Spring Mix. I gathered everything I needed to do the washing but couldn't find the light box. Turning to the Manager for help he said "Keep on looking, it's here somewhere."

Finally, I found the light box tucked away under a sink. At first glance it appeared as if it had not been used in some time. At second glance it was clear that it had been used, very recently in fact, but not as a light box. It appeared as if it had been utilized as a litter box for rodents. So I cleaned it thoroughly and covered it with several layers of shrink wrap and proceeded with my work. What happened next was something I had not experienced before nor since.

I heard some rumbling under the sink where I had retrieved the light box. Looking down I saw a long tail disappear into a pile of dirty pots and pans. Notification was given to one of the kitchen helpers who managed to extricate the creature from his hiding place and proceeded to bludgeon him or her (I didn't get a close look) to death. My desire to taste the exotic salads I had so much looked forward to quickly disappeared. Now it was time for my next encounter.

The Sushi Bar in this restaurant had once been a regular bar. Equipped with 2 televisions and high backed swivel bar stools it was a very comfortable place to be. But at this moment my comfort level had bottomed out because I was about to enter the realm of a sociopathic Sushi Chef. Fearful of identifying myself as the Mashgiach I quietly sat down in the corner, eyes glued on the TV, making sure not to make eye contact. I did not want to be there but I HAD to be there. I was told to keep an eye on him.

It was 11:30 AM, my shift ended at 4:00 PM. I prayed silently, "Please G-d, please please Ribono Shel Olam, Master of the Universe, make me invisible, keep Sushi Chef busy and may he not see me for 4 ½ hours. Amen!"

Hashem chose to not grant my wish. It wasn't because He didn't hear my prayer. It's because He heard my prayer and the answer was no. Sushi Chef saw me, Sushi Chef asked, "So you're the new Mashgiach here, huh?"

Dang, I forgot to remove my apron, it gave me away, I'm finished. I remembered what the Rabbi told me about not engaging with him in conversation. This was not easy for me being a gregarious outgoing guy. What am I going to do? Again, I silently prayed to G-d for help. This time he answered me, fully supporting my request.

"Yeah, new Mashgiach. New Mashgiach here." Hashem turned me into Raymond Babbitt, Dustin Hoffman's role as an autistic savant in *Rainman*.

Sushi Chef introduced himself as Ken and asked for my name.

"Allan, new Mashgiach. Yeah, new Mashgiach."

It worked. Ken gave me a weird look and went back to making sushi rolls.

Baruch Hashem!

After months of going from one venue to the next, for tenures lasting from 1 day to 2 weeks, I finally landed a steady 6 days a week gig. It was a non Kosher Restaurant converted to a Kosher Steak House. The new owner maintained the old staff, none of whom had any experience with Kashrut. So the other Mashgiach and I had to educate them as to what it is that we do. Three days into this new venture one of the waitresses approached me with a question:

"Rabbi, why is it that the Mashgiach on the 1st shift spends most of his time in the kitchen and most of the time you're in the restaurant?"

I replied, "That's because he's doing prep work which entails washing vegetables and checking deliveries which always arrive under his watch. In addition during his shift there's not a whole bunch of customers."

The truth of the matter is that a Mashgiach who works 2nd shift at a restaurant does not really do a lot of work. Yes, if eggs need to be inspected or if they're running low on vegetables or herbs, work needs to be done. Beside that the Mashgiach spends some time doing nothing. The problem with that is when you're doing nothing you never know when you're done.

Chapter 2

Psycho Chef

I remember way back in Grade School, around 5th grade, we were given an aptitude test which was used to determine what type of work or career we were suited for. My test results indicated that I pursue the vocation of shepherd. Fortunately my parents placed no credence in the test results and allowed me to determine my ultimate future.

The chef of the restaurant where I was employed, let's refer to him as Cheffy, had a volatile personality and was subject to drastic mood swings. He made me think that someone should devise a test to determine the probability of a career as a Chef. Here's how I think such a test would work:

1. If you like to play with knives what career would be for you?
    A. Chef
    B. Surgeon
    C. Carnival Performer
    D. Flamenco Dancer

2. If you enjoy screaming at people what career suits you?
    A. Chef
    B. Lawyer
    C. Traffic Cop
    D. Warden

3. If you have a propensity to threaten and intimidate others what career would you pursue?
    A. Chef
    B. Wrestler
    C. Middle Linebacker

D. NY Cab Driver

Cheffy would have answered A to all the questions.

Cheffy sent one of the kitchen helpers to fetch the Rabbi. When I arrived I was instructed to bring Cheffy a dozen eggs. This was my 1st request for eggs and so I had to search the walk-in cooler to locate them. When I returned to my station I was greeted by Cheffy, 12" knife in hand, menacingly waving it while screaming, "Where's my eggs...where's my frigging eggs? What's taking so long? What's your problem?" When the rant subsided I slowly looked behind me over my left shoulder, looked behind me over my right shoulder and in my best Robert deNiro Taxi Driver imitation responded, "You talkin' to me, you talkin' to ME??? " He did not quite know what to make of this. So he put down the knife and walked back from whence he came, softly mumbling something indiscernible under his breath.

One evening, after completing my shift of doing nothing in the dining area of the restaurant, I decided to take a break and do nothing in the kitchen. Shortly thereafter Cheffy came through the kitchen on his way outside for a cigarette. He ordered me to remove a very large pan from the oven. This pan contained beef ribs which had been cooking for 9 hours. I grabbed 2 pot holders and started removing the pan very carefully from the oven. The liquid was close to the top and some spilled over on my thumb and index finger as I placed it down. The pain was severe and I stuck my hand into the ice maker. Later on, one of the kitchen staff said to put ketchup on the burned areas to keep my hand from blistering.

So there I sat, left hand smothered with ketchup, and in walks Cheffy. You're probably wondering how he reacted. His reaction was predictable for a budding psychopath........laughter.

"What happened? Did a bottle of ketchup explode in your hand." He barely got the words out amid bursts of laughter.

"No, that's not what hapened" I explained."I scalded my hand doing your job" I continued, trying to evoke some guilt in him.

"Well next time don't be so stupid and use gloves, Rabbi."

"There won't be a next time, Chef. This is not the job of a Mashgiach." I sure told him! One aspect of my job is doing nothing which I do very well. Taking pans out of ovens and scalding my hand is not for me.

The next day was Friday. The restaurant was not open for business except for people who were picking up their orders for Shabbat. The only thing I had to do was be there....... and do nothing.......one of my specialties. Before I left for work I bandaged my hand with enough gauze to make the injury look worse than it was. It worked.

"Oh, my G-d", proclaimed Cheffy when he saw me. "I didn't realize this was such a serious injury."

It's quite serious, I thought to myself. So serious that perhaps I may never be able to play the tuba again.

They were only open for a few hours, just long enough for customers to pick up their orders. What happened just before closing shocked me. The chef did teshuva. He wanted to make up for what happened and I played it to the hilt.

"We have some extra food left. Would you like to take some home?"

"Yes, I would. My wife wasn't able to prepare anything for Shabbos because she was busy cleansing my hand and applying bandages and then removing the bandages before I went to work so she could cleanse my hand again and apply some Aloe Vera and then put on new bandages."

With great joy I watched as he packaged pargiot, short ribs, kasha varnishkes, gefilte fish and assorted salads into 3 shopping bags and asked if this would be enough.

"Oh, for us this is plenty but you never know who could stop by for lunch."

Two shopping bags later he asked if he could bring it to my car. I graciously accepted but I wasn't done.

"I really hate to ask for this, but do you have any extra pie? Normally we don't indulge in desserts but you know it is

Shabbos and in honor of the Holy Sabbath we should have dessert."

"Sure, we have a lovely Tiramisu and a French Silk. Which one would you like?"

"Hmmmm, that's a tough choice.......wow, I just can't decide. Let me call my wife."

"No, that's okay. You can have both."

Somehow I had the feeling that's what he would say. I played this very, very well.

Chapter 3

Bird Brain, Grill Man & Girly Man

After working 7 months at a "steady" gig I was offered a position at a fast food restaurant 10 minutes from where I lived. I jumped at the opportunity. Not only would I get home every night before 10 PM, but I would be required, when necessary, to help out on the grill. At last! My dream of working as a fast food cook had materialized.

For as long as I could remember I was always fascinated by watching grillmen work. Flipping burgers was one of the coolest things a guy could do. Although I never pursued it I knew in my heart that one day I would have the opportunity to fulfill this longing. And then, in my late 30s, it materialized.

Across the street from where I worked a family opened up a fast food restaurant/tavern. We became instant friends. The father tended to the bar business, the mother did the cooking and the 2 sons managed the fast food. I informed the sons of my desire to flip burgers and they told me that at the appropriate time I would get my chance.

Finally it happened. I was summoned across the street to help out. It had gotten very busy and they needed an additional hand. Ready to go, I arrived with an authentic chef's hat (I don't mess around), last worn at a Purim Party and an apron which had written on it Born To Grill. These preparations were made months ago in anticipation of my debut.

"Start making fries" barked the older son John. "Bring me some hamburger buns" commanded little brother Bill.

Begrudgingly I followed my orders. Maybe I have to work my way up to flipping burgers, I thought. For the next 40 minutes I made french fries and onion rings; refilled the napkins; took orders on the phone and replenished the pickles, tomatoes and sport peppers. I had to return to work soon and it didn't look like I'd be doing any grilling this day.

It started to slow down. John looked my way and said, "Okay, now's your chance. 2 burgers to go."

Hoo ha! Time to show my stuff. I took 2 burgers from the fridge and placed them one behind the other on the grill. That's how us grillmen work. Leave room at the front of the grill for new orders. 3 and a half minutes passed, time to flip the burgers. But first get the buns and put them on the grill. Flip the front burger, pat it down and now for the one behind it.

"AYYYY!!!!". The grease dripped down from the front burger and caused the flames to shoot up, burning my hand and singing the hairs as I flipped the back burger. I am holding my hand in pain while John and Bill are rollicking with laughter. "Hey grill man," chuckled Bill, "you just learned what not to do on a charcoal grill. You'll never do that again." John gave Bill a high five and I left, nursing my wounds.

That was it for Grill Man for the next 30 years. In 2015 I went to work at a small fast food restaurant. Both the owner and cook were usually there, which did not afford me much activity behind the grill. So I passed the hours doing some vegetable checking and taking money from the customers. As time went by I came to see that I was there for one reason and one reason only---keeping the owner honest and the restaurant Kosher. Let's call this restaurant Dan's Pita, named for its proprietor.

Dan's opened 2 years before I got there. The job description of their Mashgiach included delivery and shopping. This is not okay. A Mashgiach in a fleishig restaurant is never supposed to leave the premises. So when ORB discovered what the previous Mashgiach was doing I found myself with a new job. The day before I would start I stopped by to tell the owner that I would be the new Mashgiach. We know each other. He was not overjoyed to see me.

Dan used to do the catering at the Synagogue where I belonged. One year the Synagogue was having a Chanuka party at the conclusion of Shabbot. A group of us were hanging around the Shul and I heard some noise coming from the kitchen between Mincha and Ma'ariv, shortly before Shabbot ended. I entered the kitchen and found Dan and a pal placing latkes into the warmer. The latkes in the aluminum pans were warm.

"Good Shabbos guys! You're a little early, Huh?"

Dan knew he had been caught in the act. There could be no response as to why he was delivering food on Shabbos especially hot food. He explained: "I kept the latkes overnight in my van in a hotbox so it wouldn't take long to warm them up."

Why, of course, I thought, and you hired flying monkeys dressed in waiter's garb to serve the latkes with applesauce and a special monkey to avoid serving sour cream to those who were still fleishig from Shabbos.

Understandably I was not his most popular Mashgiach. He knew he wouldn't get away with any shenanigans under my watch. ORB had told me that I was sent there to straighten him out. I suspected that this was not going to happen.

Before I begin the narration of my experiences at Dan's I'd like to introduce the cast of characters along with a brief description. At first glance it appears as if these are players in a soap opera. Names have been changed to protect the perpetrators.

Headlining the cast is Dan, the owner of the restaurant. He is a very talented and creative cook who has a problem telling the truth. His motto is "Catch me if you can and if you do I'll deny it."

Next up is Tom, the grillman at Dan's. I wouldn't call him a cook but he knew how to slice the shwarma and work the grill. Tom was a visionary, he prescribed medical marijuana for himself before it became the fashion. Exactly what malady he suffered from remains to be seen.

And now for Miss Bernstein. She was quite outspoken and in a couple of weeks she earned the nickname "Miss Bird Brain." She was a good organizer and helped out when needed for catered events. In her own words, "I am a valuable member of the team. In addition to my excellent organizational skills I know a great deal about Kashrut because my Dad's Uncle had a Kosher Restaurant." It's always good to have another Mashgiach on staff.

The 1st shift and catering Mashgiach was Itzy. He was one of those Rennaisance Men who knew most things about everything. No need for Wikipedia with a guy like Yitzy around. His integrity as a Mashgiach was not what I would aspire to. He worked well with Dan.

And finally we have Miss Marcel, no typo here, MISS Marcel. She (his personal pronoun of choice) was a wonderful Chef who did catering and specialized in presentation, always making sure that the colors of the edible flowers did not clash with the vegetables. Oh, for the record, Miss Marcel felt that spices and seasonings did not need to be Kosher. This required very careful scrutiny but not TOO careful. G-d forbid Miss Marcel would feel the pressure and get a splitting headache and not be able to cook.

Within one week of my new job I had an incident which clearly illustrated what I was in for. Dan was doing catering from another location. Previously he had the Mashgiach from the Restaurant running between the 2 locations but when I came on board Dan was told he must have another Mashgiach on site while he was doing catering at the Synagogue.

It was Sunday morning, the only day of the week I opened. Dan had called to tell me he wouldn't be in until about 1:00 and the cook would be there in his place. We opened at 11:00 and a gentleman came in looking for Dan. "Is Dan here?" he asked.

"He should be here about 1:00" I replied.

"I just saw him at Beth Emanuel and he said he was coming right over."

"What was he doing at Beth Emanuel?" I inquired.

"Men's Club monthly brunch" he volunteered.

I told the cook I have to lock up for 1/2 hour and drive over to Beth Emanuel so I could see for myself what was going on.

When I got there Dan had already left, but there was Marcel, preparing omelets. I walked into the kitchen to look for the Mashgiach, only to find Miss Bird Brain cracking eggs. "Have you checked the eggs for blood spots?" I innocently inquired. She proceeded to inform me that in these modern times it's not necessary and explained why. I thanked her for enlightening me and then told her she had cracked her last egg and to go home. Next I proceeded to inform Marcel that he (she) was done for the day as I removed the butane cartridge from the burner under the omelet pan. An exchange of words ensued, mostly by Marcel, as I politely listened to his rant which included accusations of homophobia, racism (he was Caucasian) and anti Christian bias. When he was done I looked around the room and asked him if he was talking to me.

Before I called ORB I went to the kitchen to see if Miss Bird Brain   had left. As I entered Dan arrived at the same time. Miss Bird Brain had called him to report the "bust." "What are you doing?" he shrieked. "Are you insane?"

Maintaining my composure I quiety answered   "There is no Mashgiach here and I shut you down."

"We're only making omelets and we don't need a Mashgiach for that" he explained

"I don't care if you're boiling one egg, you need a Mashgiah to turn on the flame."

That's when he put it all into perspective as he told me: "Allan, you've got a big problem!"

"What's my problem?" I asked.

"You go by the book" he informed me.

I stared at him and in my softest firmest voice I replied, "No, Dan...YOU have a big problem.

The ORB was notified right away. This would not be the 1st time.

Several weeks was all I had to wait for the next encounter. When I arrived at work Miss Bird Brain and Itzy were preparing platters for a customer. The platters consisted of vegetables and wraps. None of the vegetables required checking, the eggs were hardboiled and the tuna was Kosher. Not much supervision here, but with this group you always had to be aware.

"Itzy, we ran out of tortilla wraps so I need to go get some more" announced Bird Brain.

"And where do you plan on buying them? I innocently inquired.

"Publix, they have Kosher tortilla wraps there" she responded .

"They're not Pas Yisroel, you'll have to go buy them at a Kosher Supermarket" I explained.

Miss Bird Brain was not familiar with Pas Yisroel and informed me that as long as the wraps were Kosher that's all that mattered. Besides, she didn't have time to drive 45 minutes each way to the nearest Kosher Supermarket.

"Come with me my dear" I said in my best paternal voice. "Please allow me to show you something." I pointed towards the certificate of Kosher Supervision, put my finger next to where Pas Yisroel was written and said that everything that comes out of this restaurant must adhere to this standard.

"What the heck is Pas Yisroel? I never heard of it," questioned Bird Brain.

Never one to miss an opportunity to educate another I explained Pas Yisroel in detail:

"Very simply stated, Pas Yisroel means that a Jew must turn on the oven for the baking of any product This is an ancient concept. It arose out of the following concern: Let us say that a non-Jewish girl was working at a Kosher bakery. Turning on the oven could lead to interaction with a Jewish boy which may result in social dancing and everybody knows that the next step is intermarriage. That's why we have Pas Yisroel."

Miss Bird Brain proceeded to launch into an expletive laced soliloquoy "Pas Yisroel makes no sense, it's an outdated custom, has nothing to do with Kashrut and why am I such a jerk to enforce it."

"Miss Bernstein, I agree with you on all issues except the jerk thing. Nevertheless you must abide by the rules."

Chapter 4
A Man & His Scotch

Jews are not known for being heavy drinkers. Getting "shicker" (drunk) is not a commonplace thing amongst Jews although it would be naive to say it doesn't exist. Jews have a different relationship with liquor. It's more about the quality of what they consume, not the quantity. You will not find many Shmuels or Yosefs in line at Walgreens with a couple of bottles of Jim Beam in their shopping carts on sale for $5 each. Nor will you see Yitzchak and Moshe stocking their shelves with gallon bottles of Comrade's Vodka from Kamchatka, reduced to $9.99.

Once upon a time you could identify a Jew's affiliation or family origin by what they drank. Russian Jews drank Vodka. Polishe Jews drink cheap Vodka. Hungarian Yidden drink Slivovitz. Rumanian Jews drink whatever they can steal. Galicianers drink whatever they're served. Lubavitchers drink Crown Royal aka Keter Malchut. Conservative and Reform Jews do mixed drinks. Today, things have changed.

Single malt Scotch is the liquor de jour. These Scotches are aged from 3-50 years, mostly in oak casks. All of these Scotches are Kosher. Some are aged in Sherry casks. There is a machlokes (question) as to whether or not these Scotches are Kosher. Some say yes, others say no. It depends on what Hashgacha you hold by.

A family of snow birds from Montreal, members of the Synagogue I belonged to, were sponsoring a weekend long celebration for their grandson who just became Bar

Mitzvah. They commissioned the premier caterer in South Florida to provide the food. Included was a fully stocked bar and a professional bartender. A Mashgiach's duty is to arrive when the food is delivered in order to check everything out. As long as the caterer delivers everything in closed containers, sealed with the tape of the agency providing Kosher certification, nothing needs to be checked. The liquor, mixes and garnishes, however, arrived in a separate box.

The liquor medley was quite impressive. Varieties of Vodka, Gin, Tequila, Bourbon, Liqueurs and Wines all passed the Kosher test. The only exception was an 18 year old gallon bottle of Single Malt Scotch, aged in a Sherry Cask. As a conscientious Mashgiach I removed the bottle and hid it in the kitchen. The bartender had not arrived so I would wait until he appeared to explain the absence of the Scotch.

My instinct told me that I was in for a dispute. The first clue was that all the other liquors came in regular (fifths) bottles. The gallon bottle of Scotch suggested that this was the drink of choice for the person who bought the liquor. The second issue was the difference of opinions between Kashrus Agencies concerning Scotch aged in a Sherry Cask. Some say it's Kosher, some say not. I work for ORB who holds by the latter view.

Mincha (afternoon) services began at 5:00 this winter day. At 4:55 I entered the Sanctuary to see if we had a Minyan. We were short 2 and the Rabbi asked me to go out and see if anyone had arrived. I left the Sanctuary and walked to the Social Hall where the Shabbat Dinner was held. As I entered a very tall, large man with a long black beard, attired in black suit and hat greeted me with, "Are you the Mashgiach here?" His tone of voice gave no indication that this was a man who was filled with joy at the moment.

"Yes I am," I replied, "how may I help you." Knowing full well what he wanted I awaited his answer. "My Scotch is missing, I need to have my pre-Shabbat l'chaim" he explained angrily. "Do you know where it is?" This situation was not unfamiliar to me. This man, this very large man was suffering from SMSDD...Single Malt Scotch Deficiency Disorder. He was exhibiting symptoms of Stage 1 of this malady. Unless proper action was taken things could get ugly.

Sometimes humor works to disarm an angry person. So I tried the good news/bad news routine. "The bad news is that your Scotch was aged in a Sherry Cask. Here in South Florida that is not allowed. The good news, however, is that there is a very fancy liquor store less than a block away which has a large selection of Kosher Single Malt Scotches."

This did not placate him. Instead it antagonized him as he launched into a tirade against me, Mashgichim in general, South Florida's Kosher supervision, American Conservatism and my Shul. Clenched fists, finger-pointing and snarled facial expressions made me fear for my well being. Little did I know but at the very moment this rant began the Rabbi came looking for me and heard the whole soliloquy.

"Shalom Aleichem, welcome to our Shul" greeted the Rabbi. "You won't believe this but I've got 2 bottles of unopened 21 year old Balvenie Scotch in my office just waiting for a simcha. Let's say l'chaim and start Mincha."

Baruch Hashem! The Rabbi saved my life and he knew it. "You owe me big" he whispered in my ear as we entered the Sanctuary.

Chapter 5

A Woman & Her Vodka

Oh what an event this was to be! Synagogue Beth El was honoring their Rabbi in celebration of his Bar Mitzvah. At 60 years old that's quite unusual if not for the fact that this Rabbi was born in the then Soviet Union where Bar and Bat Mitzvahs were not held. And so to commemorate this great milestone Beth El was holding a weekend long celebration in commemoration of their Rabbi attaining manhood.

Sunday night was the Grand Banquet. For starters, guests were served exotic hors d'oeuvres which included Black Sea Caviar, a true Russian delicacy. The caterer wasn't hip as to traditional Russian faire so there was no Zakuski nor Chebureki in sight. However, he did know how important Vodka is to Russian culture and the Caterer went all out with an ice sculpture fountain of Vodka. The ice was sculpted in the shape of a samovar, a sight to behold.

The presentation was exquisite. Russian Vodka was juxtaposed with the American Martini featuring all kinds of Martini mixes. There were choices of Chocolate Martini, Lemon Drop Martini and Appletini, along with Martinis in practically every flavor and color of the rainbow. Upon inspection all Vodkas passed the Kashrut test. This was not so for the mixes and Liqueurs. Six bottles which were not certified Kosher had to be removed from the bar. The bartender was kind enough to provide me with a box so I could put them away.

"Hey, where do you think you're going with that?" shrieked a voice from the crowd. I turned to see a middle aged (now that I'm 71 I consider 65-85 middle age) woman sprinting my way. Considering the 5" spiked heels she was wearing it was miraculous she was able to maintain her footing.

I politely explained that the bottles in the box were not Kosher and could not be used which is why they are being taken away.

"Honey, let me set you straight about something" she began to explain. (She called me honey. Now that we were intimate I knew we would have a meaningful conversation.)

"Most people in this Synagogue don't give a hoot about Kosher so just put the bottles back in the bar" she ordered.

"No can do" I explained.

"Can I take a peek and see what's being taken away?"

"Sure, be my guest."

She looked in the box, scrutinizing each bottle and removed one of them muttering to herself, "Oh no, not this one." She clutched it securely to her breast and proclaimed, "Okay, take the box away but I'm keeping this for myself."

"And may I ask what are you planning on doing with that bottle?" I inquired.

"Sweetheart, I'm going to give it to the bartender and have him make me my favorite cocktail, a Green Apple Martini. You look like an intelligent man honey, why even ask?" (Wow! Sweetheart <u>and</u> honey in the same conversation…we're really getting it on!) I decided to have a little fun with her.

First I explained to her that all foods at this event were provided by a Kosher Caterer who is certified by the ORB. The Synagogue, as per the contract, provided the liquor. I explained that as the Mashgiach it is my job to make sure that all bar items are certified Kosher. Martini Mama did not buy into this and so I gave her some options.

"You basically have 3 choices" I explained. "Choice #1 is that you hand over the bottle and I'll return it to the box. Choice #2 is that you have the bartender make your Green Apple Martini in a disposable cup with a lid and have him put it in a brown paper bag which you can consume in the parking lot. Maybe this could develop into a tailgate party with some friends. And choice #3 is take advantage of this wonderful opportunity G-d has given you to experience personal growth."

Choice #3 seemed to arouse her curiosity.

"How will choice #3 enhance my personal growth?" she said with smirk on face.

"Simple" I explained, "You will broaden your horizons by trying another Martini Mix and who knows………maybe you'll really enjoy it, hence you have expanded your repertoire of personal favorite Martinis. Voila! Instant self improvement!"

She stared at me, mouth slightly agape, blank look on her face and handed me the bottle. As she slowly moved away she shook her head and muttered something indiscernible under her breath. I think I made my point.

My next stop was to check out the area where dinner would be served. The caterer had arrived with the food and I needed to make sure everything was in order. I never would have anticipated what happened next.

Chapter 6

Don't Mess With My Kit Kat Bar

The banquet hall in this Synagogue was decorated very lavishly, or as it is said in Yiddish, quite *farpitzed.* Each table featured a floral centerpiece that must have extended three feet into the atmosphere. I usually don't pay attention to floral decorations but these captured my attention. Multi colored gladiolas and branches of fragrant jasmine along with ferns and other greenery caught my eye. Each table had matching napkins and tablecloths, all of different colors. Every place setting had its own vase which contained a mini orchid. This sat atop a 5 X 8 piece of parchment upon which the menu was written in impressive calligraphy. The water and wine glasses were of the Waterford variety as pointed out to me by one of the wait staff. Gold cutlery enhanced the expensive chinaware with colorful patterns. The tables were a sight to behold.

With all this glitter and glitz one thing did not escape my eye. A plainly wrapped rectangular package sat at every place setting. It certainly did not befit the extravagant décor and my curiosity got the best of me. What lay within this unobtrusively packaged parcel I asked myself. Since it did not match the rest of the table it must have been placed there by someone unaffiliated with the Caterer I surmised. Or perhaps it's a promotional piece from some vendor, peddling their wares. And then again it could be a gift from someone to the guests. Maybe it's a commemorative pen and pencil set given by the Rabbi himself and engraved with the words: Boris' Bar Mitzvah…. From Siberia to Simcha. There was no knowing what was contained within.

I decided to have a look and opened the package. Not in one hundred years would I have guessed that inside was a Kit Kat Bar. Yes, a Kit Kat Bar, this chocolate-covered wafer bar confection consisting of two pieces, each composed of three layers of wafer, separated and covered by an outer layer of creamy milk chocolate. Each finger can be snapped from the bar separately. Sounds quite delicious but it didn't fit at this elegant affair.

The good news was that they bore an acceptable Kosher Hechsher. The bad news was that the bar is Dairy and could not be served at this Fleishig meal. So I had to remove the Kit Kat Bars from the table. I enlisted the wait staff to assist me in this endeavor.

The guests had started to come in. As fate had it Martini Mama took a seat at a table where the Kit Kat Bars were being removed. She was not happy to see me. "You again" she snarled. "What are you doing now?"

"Clandestine undercover Kosher Police work" I explained. I held up one package and continued, "Someone smuggled these Kit Kat Bars into this dinner. They're milchig and the dinner is fleishig. They're outta here! End of story."

The drama was added because Martini Mama was pretty tipsy and I thought I'd have a little fun with her.

Her response was unexpected. Rather than put up an argument she grabbed her Kit Kat Bar, clutched it to her breast and proclaimed, "You're not taking this from me, it's mine…it's mine!!"

She held it as if she was protecting her first born child from being ripped out of her arms. The others seated at this table followed suit. Each one of them placed the package in their purse or suit coat in an act of defiance, deliberately denying me from making the bust. This created quite an uproar and other tables were taking   notice. The Rabbi came to investigate and I explained what was transpiring. I sensed a full blown protest about to take place but the Rabbi who was   trained   in   these   matters   stepped   in. "Ladies, gentlemen, please please calm down" the Rabbi pleaded. "These dairy candy bars were placed at the tables by mistake and can't be eaten along with the standing rib roast we're about to enjoy. So I am asking the wait staff to collect them and they will be returned to you by our valet parking service when they retrieve your cars." Calm was restored. Once again I felt safe and secure. Oh, the trials and   tribulations   a   Mashgiach   endures.

Chapter 7

Chocolate, Cholent & Chabad Chassidus

From my earliest childhood memories I can always recall having a taste for chocolate. Actually it was more than just a taste, there's a Hebrew word for it, a *teivah*. Perhaps it was a longing, an obsession. I don't really know what it was except that chocolate was irresistible to me, whenever I saw some I had to have it.

As a teenager I prided myself as having tried every chocolate candy bar on the market. Peter Paul Almond Joy, Kit Kat, Butterfinger, Peter Paul Mounds Bar, Snickers, Clark Bar, Hershey's Milk Chocolate, Nestle's Crunch, Baby Ruth, Milky Way, Hershey's with Almonds, M and Ms..........the list goes on and on.

In my 30's I had not outgrown my love for chocolate. One Thanksgiving some friends came over for dinner and brought me a chocolate covered peanut butter turkey. We already had plenty of desserts so my ex-wife put it in the freezer. Actually she <u>hid</u> it in the freezer. (one reason she's an ex-wife) In truth I forgot about it until almost 2 years later. By then it was frozen solid but there was nothing in the house to satisfy my sweet tooth so I had to have some. I had no patience to wait for it to defrost. After 2 years in the deep freeze it could not be cut so I tried shaving off pieces but that wasn't enough to satisfy my craving. So I did the only thing left to do. I placed the turkey's head between my front teeth and tried to bite its head off.

The next day I went to the Dentist to treat my wound and explained what happened. He stared at me in disbelief.

"This is physically impossible" he explained. "You're telling me your teeth could not sever the turkey's head and slipped off, driving your bottom teeth into your upper palate? The jaw is not designed to allow that to occur. Now tell me what really happened."

My dear readers, that's what really happened. The sore behind my front teeth took a week to heal. During that week I couldn't bite into anything nor chew food and so I subsisted on a diet of chocolate pudding, chocolate ice cream, chocolate mousse and hot chocolate. I was on the mend and treated myself nicely.

Time has not healed my addiction. Over the years I have experienced chocolate binge eating. In fact I have been diagnosed as a partial bulimic. Partial because I only do the binge part.

A short time ago I was assigned to work for one week at a caterer known for his exotic desserts. The timing was impeccable. Some two weeks earlier my bathroom scale gave me some bad news. My weight was 1 pound away from my panic point. To me this could potentially be the point of no return, the point where you realize you're out of control and wonder if you can ever recover. I'm a person who does not have the word quit in his vocabulary.

So here I was, two weeks into the diet, 4 pounds lighter and looking my nemesis in the face, knowing by the end of the week I would either have triumphed over my temptation or succumbed to it. It did not take long to see what awaited me. The caterer brought out two of the largest bars of chocolate I had ever seen. They must have weighed close to five pounds apiece. The next item to appear was a five pound bag of hazelnuts, undoubtedly to be mixed with the chocolate to create unimaginable delicacies designed for one purpose and one purpose only....to test my will.

Now if this sounds self-centered and arrogant it is not, Heaven forfend. It is simply a reference to Rabbi Bunim of P'shiskha, who said that everyone should have two pockets, each containing a slip of paper. On one should be written: I am but dust and ashes, and on the other: The world was created for me. From time to time we must reach into one pocket, or the other. I chose the appropriate pocket on this one.

The seduction commenced as one of the assistants broke the chocolate down into what my mind construed as being bite size pieces. Another assistant began to pulverize the hazelnuts and turn them into paste. The chocolate was to be melted down and combined with the hazelnuts. I began to drool. My resolve to resist temptation was breaking down, my *teivah* reared its ugly head, I was losing it. G-d must have seen my sorry state and sent a Malach, a Messenger, to save me.

"Mashgiach, check the barley for the cholent" the Malach spoke. According to some, dry grains need to be checked for bugs. This couldn't have occurred at a more propitious time. The cholent was beginning to take form as onions and garlic were being sautéed along with the cholent meat. This divine aroma drove me from my chocolate/hazelnut fantasies. The entire week featured many luscious chocolate creations: chocolate truffles, chocolate almond/raisin bark, chocolate fondue, chocolate covered macaroons, etc. etc. etc. With every new creation I just kept focusing on the scent of the Sabbath Stew days before. Cholent had saved the day.

On that Sabbath I was learning with a very intelligent young man, well versed in the Chabad Chassidic tradition. We were discussing the topic of *iskafia* which is best described as suppression of human inclinations. I described to him what I had experienced the past week regarding my abstinence from the chocolate. He went on to explain that when you resist and not go after a *teivah* you are bringing serious G-dly energy into the world. Lessons from chocolate, who wudda thunk it?

Chapter 8

Mashgiach versus Mashgiach

The main item on a Mashgiach's job description is the checking of vegetables. Procedures may differ from one Kashrut Agency to the next. For example, some agencies require a light box to check vegetables while others may not. Fresh cauliflower is not allowed to be used according to one opinion while another agency says that it can be checked. However, one thing does remain consistent: when you work for a Kashrut Agency, you follow their rules and procedures. That's how I look at things. For 2 days I worked at a restaurant where the Mashgiach on the early shift didn't see things this way.

This Mashgiach was also the Chef. Let's refer to him as the M/C. As I explained in an early chapter chefs can be temperamental and exhibit socially unacceptable behaviors. This one excelled at both these traits. My first day I had been at work for 5 minutes and he started up with me.

"What are you doing?" he inquired as I began the procedure for checking the bunches of broccoli that had been placed at my station.

"Checking broccoli" I responded. The wise guy, smart aleck inside me would have added "What does it look like I'm doing?" but I opted to keep my mouth shut. (one of those rare moments).

"That's not how you do it" I was advised.

"Oh really" I responded "and how, exactly, would <u>you</u> recommend I proceed?"

It was either my tone of voice, look on my face or body language that caused him to launch into a loud, angry tirade.

"Listen to me, I've been a Mashgiach for 14 years and in those 14 years I have never found 1 bug in a bunch of broccoli. Your way is wrong, you're wasting too much time, so watch closely as I show you how to do it."

After listening politely I spoke up in a quiet, firm voice before he commenced with his tutorial.

"Now you listen to me. I've been a Mashgiach for 6 years and in those 6 years I, too, have never seen a bug in a bunch of broccoli. But that doesn't mean I stop checking because I follow the procedures in the ORB Manual. Understand???"

That got him really good. He started yelling at me, waving his hands as I leaned back against the wall, arms crossed as I observed this spectacle, head tilted to the side. Finally the owner intervened and motioned for us to get out of sight of the customers witnessing the rant of this Chef/Mashgiach.

We walked to the back of the kitchen and he started up again. I counted to ten, gave him the time-out sign and interrupted:

"There's only 2 things you need to know. Number 1 is that when the clock strikes 4:00 I am the Mashgiach here and number 2 is that at 4:00 PM Eastern Standard Time you are no longer the Mashgiach but you're still the cook. (that infruriated him….chefs hate to be called cooks) As such you will bring me whatever has to be washed, it will be washed according to ORB policies and when I'm done I will place the produce into the cooler. Now if you will excuse me I have work to do." I didn't wait for his response, I wasn't interested in what he had to say, there was no desire on my part to have any communication with him.

Day 2 began much the same as Day 1 except that on this day M/C was partially correct. The previous day I was washing scallions. It had been awhile since I had done this and couldn't recall if you cut the scallion its entire length or just the white part. I knew the green part needed rinsing but wasn't sure about the cutting, so I didn't do it.

When I came to my station I noticed that the scallions I had washed the previous day were awaiting me. My intuition told me that before long I would be visited by M/C. Here he came, walking in a regal fashion, a man with a mission. He went right into it:

"Did you wash these?" he said, pointing at the scallions.

"Funny you should ask" I answered. "I was just going to ask you the same question." My philosophy is that humor is a great vehicle to break through barriers. Get a person to laugh and you can cut through resistance like a machete through noodle kugel. It didn't work.

M/C opened his daily discourse as follows: "May I show you how to cut scallions the correct way?"

"Why of course" I replied. "I'm always willing to learn how to do things right." He eyed me suspiciously. Perhaps he detected a tinge of sarcasm in my voice.

"You've got things backward. The green part of the scallion is the only part that needs cutting. Instead you cut the onion part and left the green part uncut. Now you know how to do it right."

"I beg to differ" I replied as the manual of ORB procedures for washing vegetables was pulled out of my backpack. "It says here, and I quote, 'split open entire onion.' Shall I continue?"

Déjà vu…all over again. Yesterday's scene was replayed except today's rendition was even more animated. M/C was having a bad day. Earlier in the day he got into a physical skirmish with the cook. So now he was trying to provoke me and all I did was stare blankly at him until the hissy fit subsided. After regaining his composure he reached for the scallions and told me to watch how he wants his onions cut.

Patiently I watched as he proceeded to cut and wash the scallions his way. "Now that you have observed the proper way to cut scallions you won't make the same mistake again" he proclaimed. Rather than blurt out what came to my mind I gave some thought as to what my response should be. I looked towards the back of the kitchen and pointed in that direction with my index finger and began walking there. He followed.

"Do you recall our conversation yesterday when I told you the two things you need to know?" I asked. He nodded his head. "Good, and now I'm going to add a third. Number 3 is: I go by the book. That book is the ORB Manual for Washing Vegetables. It is not your book, do you understand? So from now on you will have nothing to say to me unless it's what vegetables you need to be washed. Do you understand?"

He was uncharacteristically silent. Perhaps he actually absorbed what I said and realized the err of his ways or he was quietly planning my demise, deciding on whether to poison my falafel balls or gun me down in the parking lot. I think he wanted to get rid of me.

He got his way. The next morning I called the ORB and told them to get a replacement. When asked to explain I told them simply: "I see Kashrut in black and white, the black letters of ORB's policy and the white paper it's written on. That is my integrity. My colleague has his own policy and lacks integrity. I won't be part of that." GOOD RIDDANCE TO BAD RUBBISH

Chapter 9
Let's Make It Mevushal

Kosher catered events are generally the most favored activity in which a Mashgiach can participate. One reason is that for the most part there is no actual work. The food has already been prepared, vegetables are checked and all ingredients have been certified Kosher. So all a Mashgiach really has to do is just be there, answer any questions guests may have and be available to help out any way the Caterer requests..........to an extent. For me washing dishes, bussing tables and serving dinner is out of the question. My rule of thumb is: I won't do anything as a Mashgiach that I won't do at home. However, on rare occasions like when the Caterer is short-handed, I will clear a table or two. If this does occur and I know people at the event I make sure to tell them that if they ever mention to my wife what I was doing I will categorically deny it and accuse them as being bearers of tall tales. (I fervently hope that my wife does not read this chapter).

Another perk at working events is that you can eat very well. Caterers get to display their talents at events and reach people who have never experienced their cuisine. And so instead of brisket the menu will feature standing rib eye, baby lamb chops in lieu of braised lamb shanks and almond crusted Chilean Sea Bass rather than grilled tilapia. Once you've learned your way around the kitchen, one of my specialties, you can grab a nice piece of fleisch, a shtickle fish or a lamb chop or two when the opportunity presents itself. An experienced Mashgiach must learn to recognize these propitious moments. It's all about finesse.

Several years ago my Synagogue was having a fundraising event for an Israeli University which was simply a wine and cheese tasting. Events of this nature do not require the services of a Mashgiach. All that has to be done is check that the cheese is all Kosher and that the wine is Kosher and Mevushal. Mimimal supervision is required. However, a turn of events thrust me into action.

Thursday afternoon I received a call from my Synagogue. The wine for the event had arrived and the Rabbi asked that I come over and check it. There were two cases awaiting my inspection. The results of the inspection were not good. None of the wine was Mevushal. Let me explain why we could not use this wine.

Mevushal means cooked or boiled. Because of wine's special role in many non-Jewish rituals, the kashrut laws specify that wine cannot be considered kosher if it might have been used for idolatry. Non-Mevushal Wine includes wine that has been poured to an idol, and wine that has been touched by someone who believes in idolatry or produced by non-Jews. When kosher wine is cooked or boiled it becomes unfit for idolatrous use and will keep the status of kosher wine even if subsequently touched by an idolater. It is not known from whence the ancient Jewish authorities derived this claim. There are no records concerning "boiled wine" and its fitness for use in the cults of any of the religions of the peoples surrounding ancient Israel. Indeed, in Orthodox Christianity, it is common to add boiling water to the sacramental wine. Another opinion holds that mevushal wine was not included in the rabbinic edict against drinking wine touched by an idolater simply because such wine was uncommon in those times.

Although this does not seem relevant in the 21st Century it is tradition and Observant Jews abide by it.

So now I had to inform the fundraiser for the event, the gentleman who shipped the wine, that it could not be used. I chose my words carefully what I was going to say. I knew this information was not going to be well received.

"Hello Jeffrey, this is Allan Lieberman. I'm the Mashgiach from Congregation Beis Moshe. How are you today?"

"I was having a great day until you called," he replied. "What's up?"

Either Jeffrey was psychic or he knew that a call from a Mashgiach is not cause for celebration. My prepared speech was trashed, I just came out and said it:

"Jeffrey, we can't use the wine you sent" I blurted out. It's non Mevushal and can't be served in our Synagogue. You've got to replace it."

Jeffrey was dumbfounded. He explained that the wines chosen were from a newer winery in the Shomron Region and it was believed that the grapes for these wines were the same grapes that made the wine King David drank. In addition he paid over $25 per bottle and with shipping the cost was almost $1,000.

"Allan, you've got to figure out how we can serve this wine" Jeffrey pleaded.

So the wheels started turning. This Mevushal thing needed to be analyzed. There are restrictions as to who can handle the wine. As a Mashgiach I can certainly pour the wine but the bottle itself cannot be visible. Aha! The solution was obvious. Put each bottle into a brown paper bag and no one will know what they're drinking. After contemplating this solution for approximately two seconds I concluded that this would not work. Brown paper bags somehow would detract from the elegant orchid floral centerpieces. Should the Synagogue ever consider a tailgate party the brown paper bag option would work nicely.

No new ideas were coming my way. I called the Rabbis from ORB but they couldn't come up with any way to solve the problem. Just then Jeffrey came up with an idea.

"Allan, how far do you live from the Synagogue?" Jeffrey inquired.

"I'm 5 minutes walking distance" I responded.

"Do you have any really large pots?" he asked.

"Yes, but where are you going with this?" I replied.

"Easy---let's make it Mevushal! We'll take all the wine over to your house, we'll boil it on your stove and now it's Mevushal!"

Creative, innovative and downright brilliant, I thought, but it's not going to happen. Boiling 2 cases of non Mevushal wine was not how I was going to spend the rest of my day. Besides, I didn't think that's how you do it anyway.

Another idea popped into my head. We could move the event to someone's home. The Synagogue supports ORB policies but an individual is not required to do so. I called the Rabbi.

"Sure, Allan, go right ahead. I'll give you a list of potential members who you can call. Be sure to tell them that we're expecting over 200 people at the event and that all their plates, silverware and wine glasses have to be Kashered. (not all members kept Kosher) And remind them that the event starts about 30 hours from now." Hmmmm, something is telling me this is a bad idea. Not as bad as Jeffrey's though.

When all hope seemed to be gone I had a flash of clarity. The issue with non Mevushal wine is how the wine itself is handled. I could pour the wine into shot glasses inside the kitchen. The wine could be served to the guests who would be informed that this was just a sample. Should they want a glass of wine we would be happy to serve them. I checked it out with ORB. They said it was pushing the issue, but they could accept it.

Jeffrey was delighted. He paid me very generously where he didn't need to do so. Every year since then he does an annual event at the Synagogue and he hires me as his personal Mashgiach. Thank G-d for non Mevushal wine.

Chapter 10

Mashgiach Rating System

This is a concept I recently developed. It does not rate the Mashgiach, it rates the venue where he or she works. Basically it's for my own amusement but I would be willing to share it with anyone who asked. This is how it works:

The Mashgiach Rating System (MRS) consists of 3 categories: Venue, Personnel and Proprietor. Each is rated from 1-5 stars with 5 being the best. My rating system is purely objective, as seen through my eyes.

The main criterion for rating the Venue is the equipment. In order to work efficiently there should be a light box, a spinner, proper knives and appropriate vessels. For example, in order to check for bugs a Mashgiach needs a clear vessel to hold water which is placed on a light box. A proper working station is important. There should be a dedicated area where the Mashgiach can do their thing. If, for example, a case of Romaine Lettuce needs to be washed there needs to be adequate space to operate. Other criteria include cleanliness and temperature control. In South Florida it can get quite hot and humid so proper AC is a must.

Personnel play an important part in the MRS. It's always a plus to be with amicable people. Whether it's the Chef, Sous Chef or the Dishwasher, all people working in the kitchen will interact with one another. It's important to be respectful. Language plays a part in the rating of Personnel. In order to communicate there needs to be a commonality of the language spoken. At the very least one should have a modicum of understanding of the English language. A Mashgiach who is washing cabbage needs to ask someone what it will be used for... stuffed cabbage, cole slaw, etc. The answer will direct how the cabbage will be cut. "No hablo Inglais presents a problem.

Finally, the Proprietor is rated. Does he or she communicate with the Mashgiach; do they obey and respect Kashrut laws; do they shut down on Erevs Shabbot and Yom Tovim when they're supposed to and do they pay in a timely fashion? All these issues are considered.

To illustrate how the system works I will select a Caterer who I have worked for at least a half dozen different occasions. Sometimes it was to fill in for a day or two and sometimes for weeks at a time until a new Mashgiach could be found to replace the previous one. Once I was asked to be the permanent Mashgiach but as you will see, that wasn't going to happen.

VENUE

Let's take a look at the Venue. Their spinner, which was used to dry leafy greens, did not work. So Romaine Lettuce was dried by standing it up in a bus pan and letting the water collect at the bottom. After washing 2-3 bags of Romaine the water had to be drained or absorbed with paper towels. (not always available) This took up unnecessary time. Often the stacked leaves would fall over and had to be restacked.

Proper knives were not always available. To cut the greens off of strawberries and slit scallions lengthwise requires a paring knife.

There was only one of these which was usually in use. Butcher or carving knives were not meant for strawberries and scallions.

Paper or dish towels were a luxury. Apparently this Caterer didn't deem them a necessary accoutrement for a working kitchen. Perhaps he was an Environmentalist. After all, by doing without paper towels you could save a rain forest somewhere and maybe even prevent a garbage dump from reaching its capacity. Dish towels, too, are a menace if you want to go green. They have to be washed and as we all know those laundry detergents are putting all kinds of dreck into our oceans and waterways. Who knows? Cutting out Tide from our lifestyle could keep the Portuguese Man of War from becoming extinct.

Let me describe the so-called working station. Basic requirement #1 is a sink, a sink that works. It's important now that I restate my earlier caveat that my rating system is purely objective. I will now describe this sink through my eyes. Please keep in mind though that a denizen in a Central African village would be most fortunate to have a sink like this. For starters the hot water was dripping constantly, not a trickle, but a steady flow of hot water. No matter how hard you turned the handle it would not stop. There was no problem like this with the cold water. That's because the cold water handle was not functional. In order to get cold water you had to turn off the cold water shut off valve beneath the sink. Otherwise the cold water would be constantly running. And if that wasn't enough there was no stopper to keep the water from draining. Fortunately improvisation kept that from becoming an insurmountable challenge.

VENUE RATING *

PERSONNEL

There were 4 regulars at this venue including the chef, the sous chef, one assistant and the dishwasher. All but the dishwasher spoke English as a 2nd language but there was no communication problem. Everyone was pleasant to deal with and cooperative,

PERSONNEL RATING *****

CATERER

Normal procedure is where the ORB will tell the Mashgiach the hours he is working. It's always best to verify with the Caterer, who, in this case, lacked communication skills. Many times I would be notified in the late evening or early morning what time to report on the day of work. Normally this could create problems but I made the best of it. Fortunately the kitchen was in a Synagogue so I always was able to do my morning prayers.

The only problem was the game this Caterer played when it was time to get paid. To be fair, he didn't always do this but when he did it was annoying. His attitude was: I've got the money; you want what I've got so let me see you jump through hoops to get it. This means (1) I'm too busy to write your check now so see me tomorrow; (2) my Secretary won't be in until 4:00 so come back later; (3) here's the check but don't deposit it until 4 days from now. On occasion he'd even bounce a check. And when he did pay he'd make it seem as if he was doing you a big favor.

CATERER RATING **

Chapter 11

To Life, To Life…..
Without Slivovitz?

Liquor doesn't play as prominent a role at Bar and Bat Mitzvahs as it does at weddings. At nuptuals the Bride and Groom are constantly being feted with the traditional Champagne toast. Throughout the evening many glasses are raised to the newlyweds as liquor flows freely. Lips loosen and stories about the Bride's and Groom's past circulate freely. Great care must be taken, however, that these tales do not reach the ears of the newlyweds lest they discover the previous adventures of one another.

This is not the case at Bar and Bat Mitzvahs. Instead of meeting at the bar for another drink guests convene at the Sweet Table to sample the delicious tasties provided by the Caterer. Conversations revolve around the latest diet they're on as they nosh on mini éclairs and chocolate mousse parfaits. The topic of the young man or woman reaching a milestone on this day must wait for the speeches and candle lighting ceremony.

The Bar Mitzvah I'm about to describe was different from most. Two hours before the guests were scheduled to arrive, as the Catering Staff was setting up, a van pulled up outside the kitchen of the Synagogue. The driver, liberally tattooed along with a generous assortment of eyelid, nose, lip, tongue and ear piercings, walked into the kitchen and inquired, "Hey! Is this the Nussbaum Bar Mitzvah?"

"Yes it is" I answered "and who may I ask would like to know?"

"Hey, that's cool man. I like your style…. Who'd like to know…. Cool, you're all right, man" he pronounced. "Manny's my name." Hmmm…Manny? I wondered if this guy could be Jewish.

I couldn't resist asking. "Is that Manny, as in Emanuel?" I inquired.

"Close" he answered. "It's Manuel without the E, Manuel Luís Filipe Madeira Careiro Figo."

"That's a long name" I observed. "How do they fit all that on your driver's license?"

"There ya go again, you're a funny guy, man. My father gave me the name, he's from Brazil, that's how they do things there" he explained.

My inquisitive mind wouldn't let it go at that. "What about your Mother, did she have any say in naming you?"

"No, she just went along with my Father. He even made her convert after I was born so I would be raised like a good Catholic boy."

I already knew the answer but asked anyway. "What did she convert from?" said I.

"C'mon man, that's so uncool of you. You know it's Jewish. I've got a good friend, Jason, who's Jewish. He told me that since my Mother was born a Jew that makes me a Jew. Couldn't you tell by looking at me?"

Of course, how could I not identify a Yid when I see one? If it wasn't the *Born to Raise Hell* tattoo on his bicep that gave it away then surely it was the multiple lip rings that betrayed his Jewishness.

"Manny, I'd love to chat with you but you've got to bring in the liquor so I can check it out. Here's my card, call me so I can have you over to my house for a Shabbot Dinner."

Manny brought in the delivery, 5 cases of liquor, a rather large amount for a Bar Mitzvah, or any Simcha for that matter. Included were 2 cases of beer, one case of wine and 2 cases of assorted liquor and liqueurs. Looked to me that this was to be a shot and a beer crowd.

All but one bottle passed the Kashrut test. The bottle in question was Maraska Slivovitz. This plum brandy, as Slivovitz is called, was made in Croatia and included a Croatian Kosher Certification that was not on my approved list. To check further I called several Rabbis from ORB and none of them were familiar with this Hecksher. So I had to remove it from the rest.

It was incumbent upon me to inform the parents of the Bar Mitzvah that the Slivovitz did not make the cut. The Father had not arrived yet so I gave Mama the news. It didn't seem to matter to her but she said to please inform her husband who had chosen all the beverages.

I returned to the kitchen to help with the plating of the fish course. My job was to place an edible flower atop a piece of poached salmon lightly drizzled with a balsamic reduction. After 30-40 platings I became quite adept at this task of placing perfectly positioned petals on poached pieces of fish. Won't this make an impressive addition to my resume?

When I finished my task I washed my hands and decided to go looking for the Father. He beat me to it.

"Where's the MashgiAH?" a gentleman asked. I found it curious that this guy had to ask where the MashgiAH was considering that the kitchen was occupied by 2 African American women, an African American gentleman, a dark-skinned Hispanic dishwasher and me.

"Hi, I'm Allan the MashgiACH, how can I help you?" I suspected that the Father might have a hard time accepting the fate of the Slivovitz.

"My wife tells me that there's something wrong with the bottle of Slivovitz I purchased. What's the problem?" he inquired. From the tone of his voice, body language and unpleasant looks I prepared for what was surely coming my way.

"Most food and drink," I explained, "in order to be certified Kosher, must have an acceptable Kosher symbol somewhere in the packaging. Some food and drink does not require certification and, unfortunately, Slivovitz is not one of them."

"May I see the bottle" he asked. I showed him the bottle and pointed out the unacceptable hecksher which bore the name of **Chief Rabbi Dr. Kotel Da-Don from the Bet Israel Jewish Community of Croatia in Zagreb.**

"Can we get another opinion?" he pleaded.

"Of course we can" I agreed, "as long as that other opinion is from one of the Board Members of the Orthodox Rabbinical Board."

He turned around and left the kitchen. Under his breath I swore I heard him say, "I'll be back."

It didn't take more than ten minutes for Daddy to return. This time he returned with a Rabbi. I knew the Rabbi.

"Shalom Aleichem, Mendy. Mazel Tov!" I greeted him warmly. "Can I help you with anything?"

"Allan," he inquired, "what's the problem with the Slivovitz? I understand that it bears a hecksher which you won't accept. May I see it?"

"Sure Mendy, have a look."

I knew what Mendy was up to. He was stepping up to the plate for his friend (probably a donor) and was trying to facilitate his desire. Even though the Rabbi respected my strictness and knew there would be no negotiation he wanted to look good and so I decided to aid him in his "dog and pony show."

"Mendy, you probably know the Shliach in Zagreb, why don't you give him a call and see what he has to say?" I suggested.

To the uninitiated this would sound like a long shot. But knowing Chabad I knew that they have Shluchim in every corner of the world and since Zagreb was the biggest city in Croatia there had to be one there.

Mendy pulled out his phone to make the call but Daddy intervened. "Nah, that's all right, don't bother. It's probably the middle of the night there and besides, I can do without my shots of Slivovitz anyway" he confessed.

"Well, we sure gave it a try" I proclaimed as we gave each other high fives and engaged in a group hug.

Chapter 12

President and Precedent

The President of the Shul I belonged to called me up one December night and asked if I would be the Mashgiach at a New Year's Eve Party being held at the Synagogue. I agreed to do so and asked who the Caterer would be. She informed me and asked if it would be okay if she brought the Champagne. "Of course" I said, "just make sure the Champagne is Kosher and Mevushal."

I enjoyed referring to the 1st female President in the history of this Synagogue as "Your Highness." We had become good friends and I enjoyed teasing her. One Shabbat I was making my rounds in the kitchen, making sure everything was okay and the kitchen help knew the Mashgiach was in the building. I just happened to be there while the Kiddush Club was in session.

"Kiddush Club" is a slang term applied to an informal group of Jewish adults who congregate during Shabbat prayer services to make kiddush over wine or liquor, and socialize. Traditionally it has been a male-bonding experience, especially in the Orthodox and Conservative Jewish communities.

Her Highness, in all her splendor and glory, was in attendance. "What are YOU doing here?" I asked dumbfounded. "This is the last bastion of male chauvinism and women are not allowed."

"Says who?" she proclaimed, "where does it say that women are not allowed at Kiddush Clubs?"

"Tradition….TRADITION!!!" I belted out in my best Tevyah imitation. "Kiddush Clubs include men, whiskey, kichel and herring. Did you hear women mentioned anywhere in that description? Once you guys start showing up it will become a Ladies Tea. Within a month we'll have colored napkins, matching plates, mini watercress sandwiches minus the crusts and mixed drinks with umbrellas in them."

Before she could respond I slipped into the kitchen to check things out.

I arrived early the night of the New Year's Party to make sure everything was in order. The Caterer arrived and everything checked out. There was ½ case of Mevushal Wine but no Champagne.

The guests began to arrive. At this point a Mashgiach's job is to keep an eye out for packages, bags or containers which may include unspeakable items of the non-Kosher species. So far no such things….until Her Highness arrived.

She was carrying a bag which I suspected contained Champagne. "Happy New Year" I warmly greeted her. "Waddaya got in that bag?"

"Champagne" she replied. "Have a look."

She handed me the bag. Due to her lackadaisical response I was expecting to see bottles of Mevushal Champagne. Instead, I was shocked to see 4 bottles of Champagne, all non-Mevushal. Her look and body language spoke for itself: **NOW WHAT?** her stare and posture conveyed.

Before I could speak she proclaimed, "Don't make a big deal about this. I spoke to the Rabbi and he said it's okay, so just let it go."

The Rabbi was present and he confirmed what Her Highness had told me. Unruffled at the Rabbi's explanation I just listened. There was nothing to do. She won this battle, the war had begun.

For reasons unbeknown to me I was appointed a member of the Board of Directors of my Synagogue. It wasn't due to my financial status nor the influence I exerted in the Community. In fact it was just the opposite. As a Chicago born and raised immigrant to South Florida my social status was at the lower echelons of this East Coast Elite Enclave here in Palm Beach.

In almost four years of "serving" on the Board I had made no contributions whatsoever except for making faces and snickering during the meetings. But the day after the New Year's Party I had a sudden revelation. I could make a contribution to the Synagogue by bringing up a motion to the Board concerning the enforcement of Kashrut standards at the Synagogue. The meeting was this coming Thursday and yes, my voice would be heard and my name would appear in the Board Minutes for the first time ever!

Thursday rolled around and I was ready for my coming out event. I had told the Rabbi of my intent and he was behind me all the way. The corresponding Secretary was informed so my motion would be put on the agenda. The meeting was called to order. The minutes from the previous meeting were read and approved; there was no old business and now, after 4 years of silence, my time had come.

"Now for new business" Her Highness, the President, announced. My palms were sweating, my heart pounded, my throat was parched as I prepared to speak. As I stood up I felt my knees start to buckle and I got light headed. "How am I going to get through this" I thought. Just then the Rabbi put his hand on mine and said, "Allan, let me make an opening comment." I gave him the go-ahead.

The Rabbi was eloquent as usual. In two minutes he convincingly argued that the Shul needed strict Kosher oversight, per the rules and regulations of ORB, to be administered by me. He turned to me. "Okay, Allan, what have you got to say?"

"Let's vote!" I blurted out. Not only was the vote unanimous but it was seconded by none other than Her Highness, the very one who scoffed in the face of Kosher Law. Ahhh, victory….how sweet it is.

The meeting ended and I did not miss the opportunity to savor my success by rubbing Her Majesty's (I call her this sometimes for a little variety) nose in it.

"I'm really so impressed with you and your character" I began. "You truly showed everyone what a good loser you are." She couldn't hide her disdain as I continued. "And, of course, you learned a very valuable lesson, one you will not soon forget."

"And what might <u>that</u> be?" she asked.

"DON'T MESS WITH ME" I enunciated. Again, the sweet taste of victory.

Chapter 13

Yiddish As A 2nd Language

While working in a kitchen in South Florida one is bound to encounter an assortment of ethnic groups. Earlier I described dealing with people of Hispanic and Haitian descent. In Israeli Restaurants there are a good number of Hebrew speaking employees. Whatever the native language was these people had some knowledge of the English Language. Communication was not always ideal but one of us was usually able to express to the other what we wanted to say.

The following situation was an exception. A grocery store that I worked at hired a dish washer, Juanita, who had just arrived from Central America with not even one word of English in her vocabulary. This grocery store featured a wide variety of prepared foods which included meat, dairy, fish and pareve. On the day she began I had to explain to her that different categories of food had their own vessels and utensils and had to be washed separately from the others.

Fortunately, the Kosher food industry has its color codes which signify what the item is used for. Red signifies meat; blue is for dairy; green is usually pareve and yellow is for fish. The sinks, vessels and utensils each had colors spray painted on them to make it easy to determine what is washed where. That was easily communicated. So as there would be no misunderstanding I took a designated meat, dairy and pareve utensil in hand and proceeded to show Juanita an example of what they were used for.

I still needed to communicate verbally. Learning Spanish was not a choice I would pursue and she wasn't going to grasp English for awhile. Another option came to me.

The brisket, schnitzel, meat balls, sweet and sour chicken, etc. were in the same refrigerated section of the grocery. With red-tagged meat tongs in hand I pointed to each dish in its red marked container and said FLEISHIG. I made Juanita repeat. The same drill was repeated for the milchig and pareve foods. Each word Juanita repeated over and over again. I switched to Spanish for a moment of clarity. "Comprende?" I inquired. "Si" she answered.

Time for her first test. I pointed at all the items in the meat section, hunched my shoulders and held my palms upward with a quizzical look on my face. "Mah?" I asked with an inquisitory tone of voice.. To my delight Juanita replied, "Fleishig." The drill continued as I moved to the pareve section. A spoon was placed in the grilled peppers. "Mah?" Juanita chimed in, "Pareve." The spoon moved to the noodle kugel. "Pareve" she replied without my asking. Henry Higgins would have been proud. The opening session of Yiddish 101 was a success.

The Yiddish word for fish is *fish*. I needed something Yiddish sounding. Consistency is what I sought. I took the yellow serving spoon, pointed at the Moroccan Salmon, Sweet and Sour Fish Balls, Poached Salmon and Gefilte Fish and said, "Gefilte." Juanita repeated, "Gefilte" three times. She was well on her way.

The following day the second session of Yiddish lessons unexpectedly took place. A pizza oven had been purchased 2nd hand and needed to be Kashered The first part of the process involved the cleaning of the oven inside and out. Every corner had to be thoroughly cleansed so no residue from the pizza oven's non-Kosher days could remain. It was not necessary to provide any verbal instructions. I learned that one of the butchers spoke Spanish and he was able to relate instructions to Juanita. It was necessary that she was aware that the pizza oven had to be 100% spotless. To stress this point I called a meeting between the butcher, Juanita and myself. On the oven door there was, what looked to be, a speck of baked on cheese. Pointing at it I said, "Shmutz, no shmutz" as I gave the two thumbs down sign.

I left to check some vegetables. 45 minutes later Juanita came looking for me and motioned that I follow her. She led me to the oven, opened both doors, pointed inside and declared, "No shmutz!" Following my inspection I raised both thumbs up and concurred, "No shmutz." Fleishig, milchig, pareve, gefilte and shmutz.......that's all the Yiddish Juanita needed to know for now.

Chapter 14

Faking It--Looking Busy When You're Not

Being a Mashgiach certainly has its challenges. One of the biggest is that the Employer is not always happy that a Mashgiach is required to be there. Some may think that any of their workers can check for bugs and verify that all foodstuffs bear a Hecksher, so why do they have to pay some outsider to do this. For this reason they resent your very presence. At times I have felt as if I am entering a hostile environment.

Another item of contention originates from the reality that there is not always something for the Mashgiach to do. I have heard Restaurant Owners and Caterers complain that they're not paying someone to sit and learn or talk on the phone while everyone else is doing something. The way to avoid this is to make it appear as if you are working when you're not. Let me make this very clear---I am not advocating this behavior, I am simply holding true to the subtitle of this book which is *Tales From A Kosher Cop,* nothing more, nothing less.

The most free time a Mashgiach will experience is at a Catering Event. Ironically it pays the most.....my personal favorite gig. At most of these events the team will arrive 1-2 hours before it begins, depending on the amount of preparation required. My job is to check the facility to be sure everything in the cooking and service area is Kosher. After that's done I would light the stove and/or sternos if there's the need. Sometimes, at larger events, I would help with the plating.

From the time the guests arrive I am either in the kitchen or out on the floor where the meal is being served. If there is nothing left to do in the kitchen I might just hang with the chef, cooks and the wait staff. This provides ample opportunity for me to sample the delicacies (most importantly the desserts) and schmooze with the peeps in the kitchen. The Caterer's perception is that I am making myself available in case my services be required. I'll hold by that.

Periodic trips are made to the floor. At this point I might mention a matter of personal procedure which is my dress code. I am properly attired in a white shirt, dark pants and a sport coat. Along with my ever present yarmulke, beard and tzitzis (worn on the outside) I look like a Mashgiach. Now I have to act like one.

This outfit makes me look official. Official looking people appear to be working. Take for example an usher at an Opera or a Play. They wear their uniforms and help you find your seat and hand you a program. That's all they do except to tell you where to find the Ladies' or Men's Room. I live in Florida so there is no Coat Room. That's it. While the performance is going on they do nothing but they still are wearing the uniform…it's official…ergo they are working.

Events can last up to 5 hours, sometimes longer. Should it be buffet style I visit each station every ½ hour or so, lifting the chaffer to view what's inside, making it look like I'm doing something. Often the server will ask me what I'm doing and so I tell them: "I'm working at looking official."

Sweet tables present problems. I try to keep my distance, it's a self-control thing. It is unprofessional for a Mashgiach to eat at the event. Fortunately, "the event" does not include the kitchen so if I lose it I can always go into the kitchen and tap into the reserves. There's always an extra box of cakes, parfaits, cookies, eclairs and petit-fours there. It's my comfort zone.

All in all I spend a lot of time on my feet at catered events although most of it cannot truthfully be described as "working." But, if the event is a Kosher one which needs supervision, there must be a Mashgiach present. Hey….someone's got to do it.

The next venue which affords the most free time is a Restaurant, particularly the 2nd shift.

By the time the 2nd shift Mashgiach starts to work the washing of the vegetables should be complete. On a busy night a restaurant can run out of fixings for salads, such as

Romaine Lettuce, Spring Mix, Spinach Leaves, etc. so there may be some work of this nature. All food deliveries have been made by this time so there is no checking of this sort to do.

A Mashgiach can always spend time examining the dry goods, refrigerator and freezer. It's always a good idea to do this periodically to assure that non-Kosher items haven't found their way into the establishment. Masgiachim can always help out with small tasks they are asked to do but face it....there's a whole bunch of free time every night shift, so what's a guy to do so he'll look busy?

There are two places to spend your time, either in the kitchen or on the floor of the restaurant. There are ways you can appear to be working in each location when, in fact, there's nothing going on and there really isn't anything you can do. Still, the Caterer wants to feel that they're getting the biggest bang for their buck. With this in mind a Mashgiach must do his best to oblige.

KITCHEN The chief denizens here are the chefs, cooks and dishwashers. None of them are signing your check so you don't have to look busy for them. So the concept here is out of sight, out of mind. If by chance the owner walks in, your very presence (don't get caught sitting around reading) suggests that you're supervising someone or something. It always looks good to be wearing an apron which implies that some work is being done.

It's important to note here that in fast food restaurants a Mashgiach will spend the vast majority of his/her time in the kitchen. Perpetuating the charade of looking busy is unattainable, therefore it is incumbent upon the Proprietor to recognize that the Mashgiach will spend hours at a time doing nothing. This precludes, of course, their willingness to help out with food prep, bussing tables, etc, none of which they are required to do. If I ever decided to become a Kosher Restaurant Consultant I would advise the owner regarding this matter in this way: "Deal with it Dude."

RESTAURANT FLOOR Mostly a Mashgiach will stand around so patrons will feel secure that the restaurant is under Kosher supervision. Walking amongst the tables is always a good thing to do. It makes the Mashgiach accessible in the event someone has Kashrut questions. From a practical standpoint you can do a good deal of walking over your shift which helps to work off all the French fries and other goodies you've been devouring. (all in the privacy of the kitchen of course)

The catering commissary can afford the least or the most free time, depending on the size of the event. Either way there's no way to fake it, you're either busy or you're not. While there's cooking or preparation

going on a Mashgiach has to be present in the kitchen which is all the time.

Chapter 15
The Presidential Palace

When Donald Trump was elected President my wife gave me an excellent idea. The Kushner family, which President Trump's daughter Ivanka married into, practiced Orthodox Judaism and kept Kosher. When they visited their father's winter retreat in Mar A Lago, located in Palm Beach Florida, they would require Kosher food. My wife raised the point that they may want to have food prepared and served for them on site which would require a Mashgiach's supervision. She suggested that I contact Mar A Lago and let them know of my availability. At the time we lived in Palm Beach and I was the only Mashgiach who lived in the area.

Already I'm visualizing myself as the 1st Mashgiach for the 1st Family, presiding over Passover Seders attended by Heads of State, Diplomats as well as influential Jews from around the world. Ivanka will undoubtedly want to purchase a complete set of Passover dishes, stemware, cutlery, pots, pans, etc. It will be a breeze to *toivel keilim* with the Atlantic Ocean and Intercoastal literally two minutes away. Ahhhh, I have such grandiose plans, but to date they have yet to materialized.

Perhaps I know why. When my "application" for this gig was presented my name was probably submitted to the FBI to conduct a thorough investigation. We know all too well what the results can be from such vetting. Although I have never committed a felony nor misdemeanor, and only one moving violation in over 50 years of driving, they managed to find some dirt on me.

In my Senior year of High School I was alleged to have started a food fight in the school lunchroom. Four people claimed that I was one of the participants. And yet, these accusers could not recall during what period of lunch this occurred, what day of the week it happened and what was the Lunch Special for that day.

Further investigation revealed that in my Sophomore year of College I was appointed Kitchen Commissar of my fraternity. In that capacity I was responsible for making out the weekly menus. The cook (Ted D.Cook as he was known) was an excellent baker and one of his specialties was German Chocolate Cake. It was discovered that one year I had requested this for my birthday and that Ted called me to the kitchen to inspect his work once completed. He had to leave to go shopping and so I beckoned my roommate to have a look too. Alone in the kitchen we scraped our fingers across the edge of the cake to taste a small sample of the frosting. One scrape led to another and before long about 1/3 of the frosting had disappeared. I contend it was only 1/4 of the frosting. My roommate can neither confirm or deny since he has been in a diabetic coma since that incident. So you'll just have to take my word for it.

Another reported incident concerned the movie "Animal House" starring the late John Belushi. In this film Belushi started a food fight in the school cafeteria which turned into a riot. An accuser, who requested anonymity, claimed that I bragged about seeing this movie at least 20 times and always referred to the food fight scene. I concur with his allegations, this I cannot deny.

The events described occurred between 40 and 50 years ago. Since then I have not participated in any food fights nor have I scraped frosting from a large surface of cake. Nevertheless there are those who feel my past antics disqualify me from such a sensitive position as Mashgiach for Mar A Lago. They may have won the battle but not the war. You can't keep a good Mashgiach down.

Every job I ever had as a Mashgiach resulted from my affiliation with ORB, the Kashrut agency in South Florida where I received training and certification. But early in 2017 that changed. A friend of mine knew someone who was a member of the ritzy Mar A Lago Club. He was planning an engagement party for his son there and had commissioned a caterer from New York to provide the food. The caterer suggested that he use a local Mashgiach and so I got the call.

The family planning the party lived in an exclusive area of Great Neck, New York and could afford the best that money could buy for their son's and future daughter-in-law's party. The party itself was not held in Mar A Lago proper but rather in a posh Oceanside setting they owned across the street.

There was no direct entrance into this Oceanside area so I pulled into the main entrance and continued driving until a member of the security detail signaled for me to stop. Before I could open the door to my car my vehicle was surrounded by 4 burly men with close cropped hair, dark glasses amid expressionless faces. I froze, not knowing whether to get out of the car or surrender. One of them motioned for me to roll down the window.

"Can we help you?" he asked.

"Yes" I replied, "I am here to provide the Kosher Supervision at the engagement party."

He pointed toward an open area near the entrance and told me to park there.

"Proceed down the path until you come to the tunnel that

will take you under the street to the Beach Club" he advised. "Any questions?"

"Why yes" I thought, "can you tell Donald I'd like to talk to him about hiring me as the official Mar A Lago Mashgiach?" Fortunately, for one of those rare times, I was able to stifle myself and didn't allow my thoughts to become words. With tongue firmly in control I proceeded to the venue.

When I got there I realized that this gig would be like no other I had ever experienced. The best way to describe the scene was that it looked like a miniature food court in a shopping mall. At one end of this area there was a tent which housed displays of what appeared to be Middle Eastern salads and mystery mixes of indiscernible "things." Upon inspection I soon discovered that this was not Kosher.

There were 3 bars, each with its own specialty: a Martini Bar, a Single Malt Scotch Bar and a Beer Garden. Half of the mixes were not Kosher; most of the Scotches were aged in Sherry Casks and a few of the Beers contained flavorings, making them unacceptable.

Finally I came to a Kosher Oasis in the Sea of *Treif.* The Caterer was unpacking the truck that had completed its 1,200 mile trek from Queens NY to Palm Beach FL. In addition to the prepared foods and raw meats the truck load included the BBQ grills on which the fleish would be prepared. All the edible contents were properly sealed and the grills were verifiably Kosher. The dishes, bowls, knives, forks and spoons were all disposable. Serving bowls, trays and serving pieces were plastic so there were no problems here, but what was I to do with the other stuff?

This affair was not under ORB Supervision so I had to reach out to the New York agency who was paying me. The only problem was that it was Sunday and they're closed. Maybe the Caterer would have a home number of one of their Rabbis. No such luck. Being a Mashgiach means that sometimes one has to rely on being logical and using their common sense. This was one of those times.

So I reasoned this one out. The host of this party hired a Kosher Caterer and other vendors to provide food and drink. I was only responsible for supervision and insuring the integrity of the Kosher food. A comparable situation came to mind—a Stadium. Many ballparks around the country have Kosher concessions right alongside pizza, popcorn and hot dog stands. Marlin's Stadium or Mar A

Lago Beach Club, what's the difference? Good reasoning or rationalization? Either way it was okay by me. It's just too bad President Trump couldn't have shared it with me.

Chapter 16

Camera Man

During my career in Kashrut Supervision I have had the pleasure to work alongside many wonderful men and women as well as others who I looked forward to forgetting. Amongst the former group I have made several friends. One of them I like to call Cameraman.

Cameraman and I first met when we worked together at a new Kosher Restaurant. He had the early shift and I had the late one. We bonded very quickly due to our mutual feelings towards the owners. We also had the same attitude towards Kashrut in general. Neither one of us saw grey areas in the laws a Mashgiach must follow. No technicolor here, folks, we only saw Kashrut in black and white.

At the "changing of the Mashgichim" (when his shift ended and mine began) we reviewed our experiences and incidents with the proprietors. In short, they were not masters of human relations. They tried to intimidate us and showed no respect for us or the ORB. Both Cameraman and I were experienced Mashgichim in our 60's and did not allow them to affect our work. At times they had to be reminded that although our checks were signed by them we worked for ORB and that is who we take direction from. We were telling them in a nice way to shut up and mind your own business. It worked, they backed off.

A few years later I get a call from Cameraman. He heard that I was working at this new Grocery Store and called to tell me about the management. There were some similarities with the Restaurant described above. It took less than a week to verify. I was working the 2nd shift except for Fridays when I opened at 6:30. It was agreed and understood that once I finished setting up what needed to be done I could daven Shachrit, the Morning Prayers. This Friday was Rosh Chodesh, the 1st day of the new month, and prayers were longer than usual. I headed to the break room to begin.

Upon completion of my prayers the Manager entered the room. He explained that it was their policy to give each employee a half hour break during the day which would be deducted from their pay. I acknowledged that I was aware of this. He continued:

"I'm not calling you a thief but your break lasted 50 minutes today. You're only entitled to 30 minutes."

When someone begins a sentence "I'm not calling you a thief" they ARE calling you a thief. I decided then and there that this environment of distrust was not one I cared to dwell in. My resignation was submitted that day.

By now you're probably wondering why Cameraman is referred to as such. Let me explain. Some time after I left the Grocery I just described there was a change in management. My friend Cameraman was working the morning shift and described the working conditions as tremendously improved. He did note, however, that there was a language barrier which resulted in some very strange signage on labels which were documented with his camera. I have the pictures to verify. Some of these things you just can't make up.

Here are some examples:

Fresh Sweet Breads Beit Yosef Glatt Kosher—this appeared on a container of potato salad......must have cow brain flavoring

Special Matjes Herring Pas Yisroel---herring's raw, this must mean a Jew CAUGHT the herring---makes sense to me!

Mushroom Bourekas Round Challah---looks like Challah but smells like mushrooms......hmmm....which is it?

My colleague Cameraman has documented several Kosher "indiscretions" at this grocery. If I were a betting man I would wager that this place is not long for the Kosher world.

Chapter 17

Religion, Politics and Kashrut

Among the many things I learned from my Father, alav ha-shalom, was to refrain from discussing Religion and Politics. My Dad had his reasons for this. He knew that discussing Religion and Politics will often lead to an argument and he didn't like to get into arguments unless he knew he could win. Also, he was well aware of the fact that in these types of discussions you rarely will change another's opinion so why bother. Perhaps another reason was that My Father, Pesach ben Leibl, was not a religious man and probably couldn't hold his own with someone who was. Same goes for Politics. He didn't seem to care much about it so I rarely heard any conversations in my upbringing of a political nature. But I do recall one family discussion which included both Religion and Politics.

The year was 1956. The Democratic candidate for President, Adlai Stevenson had just lost the election for the 2nd time to the Republican Dwight D. Eisenhower. Both of my parents were visibly upset and I asked my Dad why this bothered him so.

"Because the Democrats lost again" he answered.

"Who are the Democrats and why are you so upset?" I inquired.

My Father was a patient man and also very practical. He decided against getting into a political discussion with a 9 year old and gave me the following answer:

"Allan, I'm upset because I'm a Jew and Jews are Democrats so that's why I'm upset."

I got it, this made perfect sense. At the age of 9 the only thing that really mattered to me was baseball. I played it, I watched it, I listened to it. And when it was too cold to do any of these things I would read about it. So I was able to understand my Dad's answer through the lens of a baseball fanatic: When my beloved Chicago White Sox lose I get upset just like Pesach ben Leibl gets upset when the Democrats lose. I dig it!

Let me make a point about my Father's statement. I believe he was referring to engaging in discussions with people who sit on opposite sides of the fence than you. Religious conversations with like-minded people can be very gratifying and supportive of your belief system. Political discussions with fellow ideologues can fortify your hatred of the other side and bonds you with others. Sad but true.

If my Father were alive today I am sure he would give his oldest son permission to add another topic you don't get into discussions about, Kashrut. Unlike Religion and

Politics you shouldn't discuss Kashrut even with people who agree with you on most matters of this topic. Let me explain why.

There are different ways to wash vegetables and herbs to check for bugs. Some use thrip cloths while others use a light box. Some add dishwashing detergent to the water, others add vegetable wash, bleach or even salt. It's not a matter of right or wrong, it depends on who you learned from and what is the tradition. There are hundreds of certified Kashrut Organizations in the United States. They usually hold by the custom of one of the 5 major Hashgachas who publish manuals on washing produce. You can't go wrong this way.

Although some practices may differ they all agree on this: The leafy parts of strawberries must be removed. That's because the greenery is where the bugs hang out. My wife and I were invited to Lunch at the home of a Rabbi in our community. For dessert the Rebbetzin served a yummy looking dessert which included strawberries that had not been trimmed of their greenery. As I removed the strawberries from the cake someone asked if I didn't like strawberries. I foolishly responded that if the greens had been removed I wouldn't have to do this and explained the proper way of washing. Well..........this got back to the Rebbetzin and as a result we were never asked back.

THAT'S why you shouldn't get into discussions about Kashrut. My Father would have agreed.

Another incident occurred at a Synagogue Shabbot Lunch. A famous Rabbi was speaking there who I wanted to hear. Since the locale was 20 miles from home I needed a place to stay. The Rebbetzin was very accommodating and found me a place to stay. The lunch was beautifully catered. Everything was going smoothly until dessert was served.

Once again I discovered strawberries, greenery intact, in the fruit salad and spoke to the Rebbetzin.

"Who catered this delicious lunch?" I asked. She gave me the name and I should have let it go at that. But noooooooo....I had to explain why I asked.

"I need to call to speak with their Mashgiach. He or she is probably inexperienced and doesn't know how to properly check strawberries."

"And how DO you check?" asked the Rebbetzin sarcastically. I sensed that she was upset as I explained the proper way to do so according to ORB. That's when the fruit hit the fan.

"For your information, Mr. Lieberman, (5 minutes ago I was Allan) the fruit was prepared by me with the help of other women and that's how we do it here. I don't care what ORB does, we do it MY way here in MY Shul."

Lesson learned. No more discussions about Kashrut, especially with Rabbis and their wives, especially when you're eating at their home or at their Shul.

EPILOGUE

Working as a Mashgiach has been a very gratifying experience. I have met many wonderful people; watched some great chefs at work; accumulated some delicious recipes and most important, did my best to uphold the strictest Kosher standards wherever I worked.

For every story told in this book there are many Restaurants that have no story. For every catering incident related in my tales there are numerous venues with no incidents. And for all the experiences I encountered there were many, many more with nothing to write home about. And so I thank G-d for the stories, incidents and experiences I have shared with you for without them there would be no book!

And remember, whenever you're in a Kosher Restaurant or at a Kosher event and you have a Kashrut question don't be shy. Gather those at your table, stand tall, click on your glass do get everyone's attention and in a clear firm voice proclaim in unison: WE WANT MASHGIACH NOW!

GLOSSARY
(some definitions taken from Kof K Kosher Glossary kof-k.org)

Bar Mitzvah
Literally *son of Mitzvah*, a celebration where a 13 year old boy becomes a man

Baruch Hashem
Literally *Thank G-d*. Ask a Jewish person how they are and they will say Baruch Hashem instead of telling you all the details of what's goimg on in their lives. Saves a lot of time. Abbreviated *BH*

Chabad
Also known as Lubavitch, an acronym for chochma (wisdom), binah (understanding) and da'at (knowledge). Lubavitchers say *BH* a lot

Challah
Commonly known as a braided egg bread, traditionally eaten on the Sabbath or Holidays. Actually *challah* is the small portion of the dough that is set aside for an offering.

Chassidus
The teaching of Chassidic philosophy, brought to light by the Ba'al Shem Tov. Its basic tenet is to serve G-d with joy. Maybe this is why Chassidim like to say l'chaim. (at least the ones I hang with)

CHK
Crown Heights Kosher Supervision or Chesapeake Energy

Corporation if you're into the stock market..

Cholent
Sabbath Stew. Consists of beans, potatoes, barley, onions, garlic, meat, etc. slow cooked overnight and served on Shabbat.

Daven
Pray

Dreck
Yiddish word from German word meaning manure or dirt. Refers to something of low worth or quality, usually merchandise.

Farpitzed
All dressed up, lots of makeup jewelry and accessories. Envision Zsa Zsa Gabor.

Fleishig
Yiddish word meaning any meat or fowl product.

Gefilte Fish
Literally *stuffed fish*. Made from a poached mixture of ground fish. traditionally eaten by Ashkenazic (Eastern European) Jews. Sephardic Jews (Spanish or Portguese descent) don't know what they're missing but they get to eat rice & beans on Passover.

Glatt Kosher
The word "glatt" actually means "smooth" in Yiddish, and refers

To the lack of adhesions on the lungs of the animal. However certain types of adhesions are allowed and the meat is still deemed Glatt.

Hashem
Literally *the name*. G-d's name is not to be said in vain so Hashem is used instead.

Hashgacha
Supervision. Commonly used to refer to rabbinic supervision or a Kosher supervising agency

Hecksher
Rabbinical product certification, qualifying items (usually foods) that conform to the requirements of Jewish law.

Iskafia
Literally subjugation – is the practice of stifling one's instinctive drives through self denial. Personally, I practice iskafia by limiting my desserts to 1 serving. Hey…it's a start!

Kasha Varnishkes
Traditional Jewish dish that combines kasha (buckwheat groats) with bow-tie pasta. Kasha varnishkes go with everything.

Kashrut
Term related to aspects of food preparation according to Jewish law

Keilim
Vessels

Kiddush
Literally "sanctification" it's a blessing recited over wine or grape juice on Shabbat and Jewish holidays. The custom of some is to say Kiddush on hard liquor during certain Holidays and to drink the whole cup. *__WARNING—don't try this at home!!__*

Machlokes
Disagreement or dispute usually pertaining to Jewish Law. Rabbis Hillel and Shamai were known for this.

Mah
Hebrew for "what"

Malach
Hebrew word for "messenger." In Jewish lore a malach was an angel.

Mashgiach
The supervising / inspecting Jew. The *mashgiach* supervises food production to ensure that the food, venue and utensils are Kosher.

Milchig
Yiddish word used to indicate dairy designation and any product which contains dairy ingredients.

Mincha
The afternoon prayer service in Judaism. Mincha literally means

"gift," referring to the meal offerings that accompanied the sacrifice in the Temple.

Minyan
A gathering of 10 men 13 years of age or older required for Jewish Prayer and other obligations according to Jewish law. Reform and Conservative Judaism allows women to participate. Humanists do whatever they want so who cares? I don't have to be politically correct because Humanists won't read this book anyway.

Motzei Shabbos
The going out of the Sabbath referring to the evening after Shabbos has ended. Typically this is 45 minutes after sundown.

Pareve
A Yiddish word meaning neutral, containing neither dairy nor meat ingredients. Also spelled parve.

Pargiot
Dark meat from young chickens---yummy!

Pas Yisroel
Bread or pastry products that a Jew has assisted in baking either by lighting the fire, putting the food on the fire, or adding heat to it.

Pulkeh

Chicken leg or drumstick, usually refers to chicken.

Shabbos
Hebrew for Sabbath. Shabbos is the Ashkenazic pronunciation. Sephardic (spoken in Modern Hebrew) say Shabbat. Either way it's the holiest day of the week.

Shachrit
Morning prayer

Shaliach
A Jewish emissary, most commonly associated with Chabad.

Shalom Aleichem
This is how one Jew may greet another. It means *peace be upon* you. The one being greeted will respond *Aleichem Shalom* which means *upon you peace.* This is not dyslexia, it's tradition

Shicker
Drunk, often occurring on Purim & Simchat Torah.

Shmutz
Dirt. Derivative adjective is shmutzik.

Shomrim
Plural of *shomer,* Hebrew for guardian

Shor Habor
Glatt Kosher Hecksher

Shtickle
Yiddish for a small amount, a little

Simcha
Joyous event

Toivel
To immerse utensils used in food consumption or preparation into a *mikvah* (ritual bath) so they can be used in a Kosher kitchen.

Tzitzis
The word *tzitzit* is literally defined as "**fringes**," and refers to the strings attached to the corners of the *tallit*, the Jewish prayer shawl It also refers to the poncho-like mini-*tallit* that is worn throughout the day, often under a shirt.

Made in the USA
Middletown, DE
27 May 2019